j551.5
P29m

W9-DIB-756

DETROIT PUBLIC LIBRARY

CONELY BRANCH LIBRARY
4600 MARTIN AVENUE
DETROIT, MICHIGAN 48210
898-2426

DATE DUE

JUL 0 7 1995

JAN 2 7 1996   MAY 07

APR 0 8 1996

NOV 2 9 1997

APR 0 4 1998

OCT 1 3 1998

JUN 2 3 1999

                    JUN

APR   05

                              10/07

BC-3

Meteorology

Graham Peacock

Thomson Learning • New York

Titles in the series:

ASTRONOMY • ELECTRICITY • FORCES
GEOLOGY • HEAT • LIGHT • MATERIALS
METEOROLOGY • SOUND • WATER

First published in the
United States in 1995 by
Thomson Learning
115 Fifth Avenue
New York, NY 10003

First published in 1994 by
Wayland (Publishers) Ltd.

U.K. version copyright © 1994 Wayland (Publishers) Ltd.

U.S. version copyright © 1995 Thomson Learning

Library of Congress Cataloging-in-Publication Data
Peacock, Graham.
  Meteorology / Graham Peacock.
     p.   cm. – (Science activities)
  Includes bibliographical references and index.
  ISBN: 1-56847-194-7
  1. Meteorology – Juvenile literature. 2 Meteorology
– Experiments – Juvenile literature. [1. Meteorology
– Experiments. 2. Experiments.] I. Title. II. Series.
QC863.5.P42   1995
551.5 – dc20   94-30607

Printed in Italy

Acknowledgments
The publishers would like to thank the following for allowing their pictures to
be used in this book: Tony Stone Worldwide *cover (top and middle)*, p. 5, p. 12;
Zefa p. 9, p. 11, p. 22. All commissioned photographs are from the Wayland
Picture Library (Zul Mukhida).

All artwork is by Tony de Saulles.

Contents

Words that appear in **bold** are explained in the glossary
on page 30.

Clouds

All weather starts with the sun. The sun warms some parts of the earth more than others, which causes winds to blow. The sun's heat evaporates a huge amount of water from the oceans; this vapor forms clouds and falls as rain. Extremes of weather can be exciting and terrifying.

An electrical storm is an impressive sight, yet a lightning strike can bring sudden death and destruction. In some parts of the world, like Australia's outback, the weather rarely changes. But in other parts, where enormous **air masses** mix, the weather is difficult to predict.

Cloud types

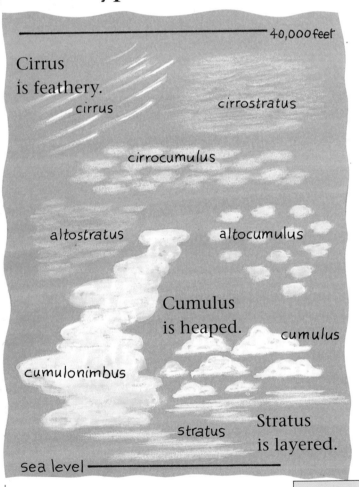

40,000 feet

Cirrus is feathery.

cirrus

cirrostratus

cirrocumulus

altostratus

altocumulus

Cumulus is heaped.

cumulus

cumulonimbus

stratus

Stratus is layered.

sea level

Stratus clouds bring light rain, sometimes for long periods.

Cumulonimbus clouds bring short periods of heavy rain, thunderstorms, and **lightning**.

Cloud watch

You will need:

◆ a large sheet of paper ◆ a ruler ◆ a pencil

1 Make a chart like the one below.

2 Look at the sky every day and record the main cloud type.

3 Estimate the fraction of the sky that is covered by cloud. Shade in that much of the bar for that day.

4 Record the main type of weather in the fourth column. Is it sunny, raining, or cloudy?

Day	Type of cloud	Fraction of sky which is cloudy	Weather (fair, sunny, cloudy or rain)
Monday	cirrus		
Tuesday	stratus		

Clouds are masses of tiny water droplets. They form when damp air becomes cool.

Clouds sometimes form in bathrooms when the air is cool and damp.

Making clouds

Warning! Take care with hot water.
Ask an adult to help.

You will need:
- a large glass ◆ a plastic pot
- two ice cubes ◆ hot tap water
- a thermometer

1 Fill the plastic pot
   with ice cubes.

2 Put 1 – 2 inches of
   hot water into the glass.

3 Rest the pot on
   top of the glass.

4 Watch the clouds form.

5 Lift off the pot and watch the
   clouds swirl out of the glass.

This photo shows masses of clouds over the rain forests of Africa. Notice the clear skies over the Sahara Desert in north Africa.

Watch the clouds swirl around in **convection currents**. The hot air rises. When it touches the pot it cools and moves downward.

rising, hot water vapor

falling, cooled water vapor

hot water

Find out:

What is the lowest temperature the water can be to make clouds? Use the **thermometer** to find out.

Rain

Make a rain gauge

You will need:

◆ a plastic soda bottle ◆ scissors ◆ a brick ◆ tape
◆ a small plastic ruler ◆ paper and colored pencils

1 Ask an adult to cut the top off the bottle to make a funnel. Rest the funnel in the bottle.

2 Tape a ruler to the side of the bottle to show the level of any liquid inside.

3 Tape the bottle to a brick to keep it upright.

4 Put the rain gauge outside to collect rainwater.

5 Make a bar graph to show your results.

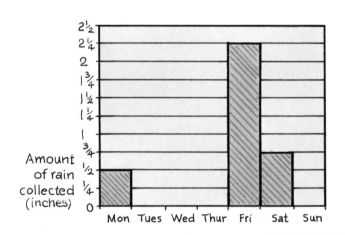

Rainfall totals

Rainfall totals are recorded in inches by **meteorologists**. They show the depth of rainwater that would be left on the ground if none ran away or soaked in.

Did you know?

Calama, in the Atacama Desert of Chile, has had no rain for several hundred years.

The highest rainfall in one day was over 72 inches, on Reunion Island in the Indian Ocean.

6

What happens when rainwater hits the ground?

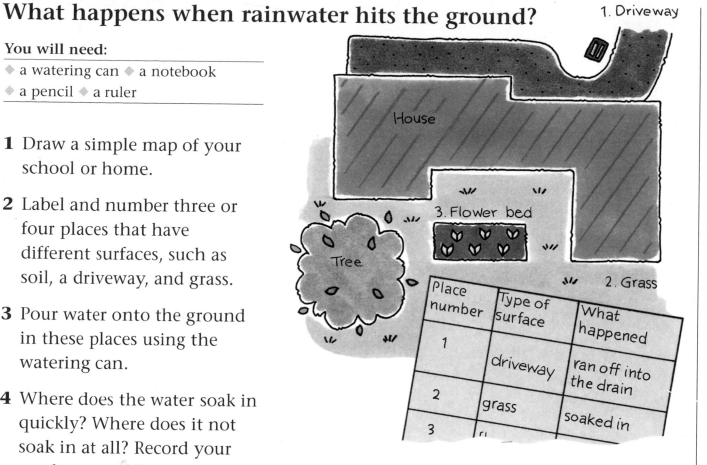

You will need:

◆ a watering can ◆ a notebook
◆ a pencil ◆ a ruler

1 Draw a simple map of your school or home.

2 Label and number three or four places that have different surfaces, such as soil, a driveway, and grass.

3 Pour water onto the ground in these places using the watering can.

4 Where does the water soak in quickly? Where does it not soak in at all? Record your results in a table, as shown.

5 What difference does a sloping surface make?

Place number	Type of surface	What happened
1	driveway	ran off into the drain
2	grass	soaked in
3	fl	

Almost all the rainwater in cities and built-up areas has to be drained away in pipes because water cannot soak into hard surfaces.

Rainfall around the world

You will need:

◆ a world atlas ◆ newspapers

1 Compare the rainfall of these three places on the bar graphs.

Which place has virtually no rain?

2 Find each country in the atlas and compare their positions in the world.

3 Look at the weather reports in the newspapers. Find places with completely different weather to your own on the same day.

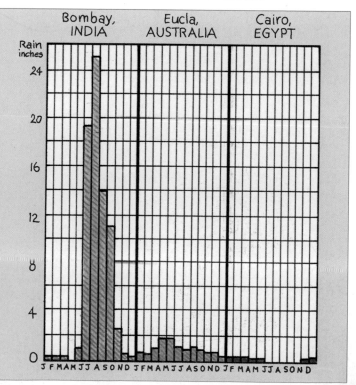

Temperature

How much temperature change is there each day?

You will need:

◆ a thermometer ◆ a sheet of paper

1 Place the thermometer in a sunny place.

2 Record the temperature every two hours throughout the day.

3 Draw a bar graph to show the temperature change.

4 Find out if there is much difference during the day between two sides of a wall. Choose a wall which gives shade to one side.

5 Repeat this on a cloudy day. Is there less temperature change when it is cloudy?

Clouds stop some of the sun's rays reaching the earth. There is less temperature change on cloudy days than on sunny days.

In the shade

Meteorologists almost always measure temperature in the shade, using a weather instrument shelter with the thermometers inside. The shelter has slats in it which lets the air move around but gives shade to the thermometers. All meteorologists use these shelters so that their temperature readings can be compared fairly.

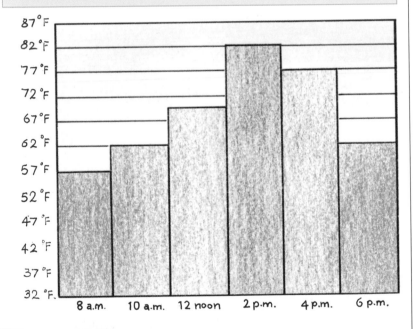

Data logging

Weather is recorded while we sleep. Computers have sensors attached to them that record all aspects of the weather, 24 hours a day.

8

Why are south-facing slopes warmer in the northern hemisphere?

You will need:

◆ a flashlight ◆ a small cushion ◆ a dark-colored towel or a piece of cloth ◆ 2 small squares of paper

1 Make a low hill by putting the cushion under the towel. Using the paper squares, label one side of the hill "N" (north) and the other side "S" (south).

2 Shine the flashlight onto the south-facing slope from the south. Notice how the beam is concentrated.

3 Keeping the light at the same angle, move it up until it shines on the north-facing slope. Notice how the beam spreads out.

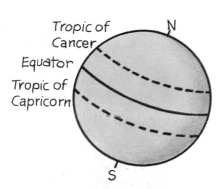

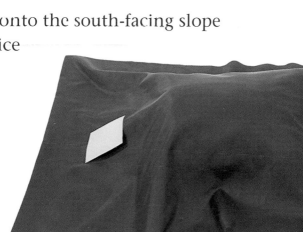

In Germany, grapes grow well on south-facing slopes.

South-facing slopes are warmer in the northern hemisphere because the sun's rays shine from the south, so they are more concentrated on south-facing slopes. In the southern hemisphere, north-facing slopes are warmer.

North of the Tropic of Cancer, the sun always shines from the south.

South of the Tropic of Capricorn, the sun always shines from the north.

Frost and snow

What happens to plants in freezing weather?

You will need:

◆ a freezer ◆ cuttings from soft and woody plants, e.g. a spider plant and holly or eucalyptus ◆ 2 plastic bags

1 Put the soft-plant cuttings in one bag. Put the woody-plant cuttings in the other bag.

2 Put both bags in the freezer for four hours.

3 Predict which plants will be badly damaged by the cold. Check your results.

Tender plants, like spider plants, cannot survive freezing. The water inside them expands as it turns to ice. This breaks down the plant's cells.

Expanding water

You will need:

◆ a freezer ◆ a plastic bottle ◆ tap water

1 Completely fill a plastic bottle with water and screw the top on.

2 Dry the outside and put it in the freezer for two days.

Plastic splits as water freezes and expands as ice

This is what happens to frozen water pipes.

Breaking up mountains

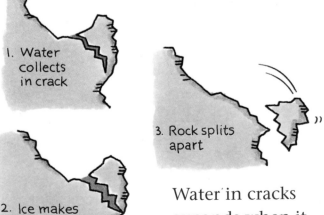

1. Water collects in crack

2. Ice makes crack bigger

3. Rock splits apart

Water in cracks expands when it turns to ice.

What shape are snowflakes?

You will need:

◆ a compass ◆ a pencil
◆ paper ◆ scissors

1 Use a compass to draw a circle. Then cut it out and fold it.

2 Fold the half circle into a triangle by making two folds.

3 Open the paper out. Make sure you have six sharp folds right across the paper.

4 Cut out a triangle from between each fold.

5 Fold the paper in half again and cut zig-zags along each arm of the shape.

6 Open the shape out to form a snowflake crystal.

Snowflakes are crystallized water. Every flake is different, but each one has six arms or sides.

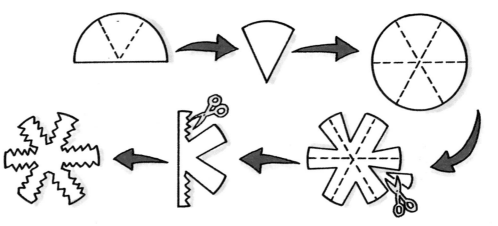

Hailstones

Hail is formed when water in a cloud freezes into ice pieces. These pieces are blown up and down between the warm and the freezing air of the cloud. The number of layers of ice on the hailstone shows how many times this has happened.

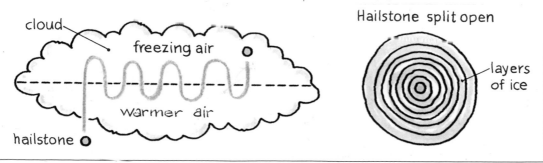

Did you know?

In 1985, 246 people were killed in India when they were hit by large hailstones.

11

Damp air

Turning water vapor to liquid

You will need:

- a metal can ◆ ice cubes ◆ food coloring
- white blotting paper
- tap water

1 Half-fill the can with ice cubes and water. Add three drops of food coloring.

2 Watch water vapor from the air condense on the outside of the can.

3 How do you know that the water hasn't simply leaked out of the can? Test it with the blotting paper.

What is dew?

Dew is formed when some of the **water vapor** in damp air cools and **condenses** on grass and trees.

The temperature at which this happens is called the dew point.

What is mist?

Mist forms when some of the water in damp air cools and condenses into tiny droplets that hang in the air. Mist is a form of clouds at ground-level.

Mist becomes fog when you cannot see anything over half a mile away.

Cool, damp air is heavier than warm air, so it sinks to the valley floor.

Work out the dew point

You will need:

◆ a metal can ◆ ice cubes ◆ a thermometer
◆ a notebook ◆ a pencil ◆ tap water

1 Fill the can halfway with cold water.

2 Add ice cubes to the water a few at a time to cool the can.

3 Leave the thermometer in the can and watch the temperature and the outside of the can. Write down the temperature at which dew begins to condense on the outside of the can.

The temperature of the dew point is a good guide to the humidity of the air. On sticky days, the dew point will be high. On clear, comfortable days the dew point will be low.

Smog

Smog is a mixture of smoke and fog. Dense smog forms in cities if lots of wood and coal are burned. In 1952, 2,850 people died in London, Great Britain, due to causes linked to smog.

Work out the visibility each day by noting which distant landmarks you can see. Both smog and fog affect visibility.

Making smog

Warning! Ask an adult to help you.

You will need:

◆ a small candle ◆ a jelly jar
◆ a notebook ◆ a pencil

1 Ask an adult to light the candle and burn it for a few minutes.

2 Place the jar over the candle.

3 Write down all the things you notice.

What do you notice about the inside of the jar?

The flame of the candle produces water vapor in the jar. This condenses on the inside of the jar like smog.

13

The atmosphere

The atmosphere is the mass of air that surrounds the earth. It is made up of different layers, but most of our weather comes from the lowest layer, called the **troposphere**. The troposphere is only about 6 miles deep.

Does air have weight?

You will need:

◆ a coat hanger ◆ 2 balloons ◆ string
◆ masking tape ◆ a pin
◆ a pencil

1 Inflate and knot both balloons.

2 Tie an equal length of string to each balloon.

3 Put a piece of masking tape on the side of one of the balloons.

4 Tie one balloon to each side of the coat hanger.

5 Hang the coat hanger from a pencil and adjust the balloons so that the coat-hanger balances.

6 Ask a friend to prick the balloon through the masking tape so that it deflates slowly. Watch the coat hanger.

The balloon full of air now weighs more than the empty balloon.

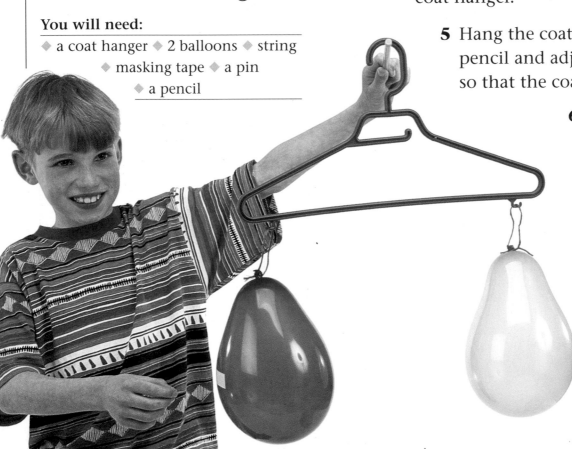

Did you know?

One cubic yard of air has a mass of about 2 pounds. The weight of the air in an average classroom is about 150 pounds.

All the air in the atmosphere has a mass of about 5 quadrillion tons: this is equivalent to the mass of nearly a quadrillion elephants.

14

Air pressure

You will need:

◆ a coffee mug with a handle ◆ a piece of cardboard, a little bigger than the mug's rim ◆ a large basin ◆ tap water

1 Fill the mug to the brim with water.

2 Place the cardboard on top and press it down firmly.

3 Hold the mug by the handle with one hand, and keep the cardboard pressed to the mug's rim with the other. Hold the mug over the basin and turn it upside down.

4 Now take your hand away from under the cardboard. What happens?

The force of the **air pressure** pushing the cardboard up is more than the force of the water pushing it down.

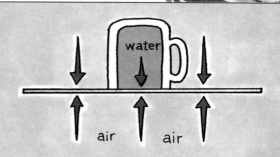

The air in the atmosphere presses in all directions.

Moving air

1 Hold two pieces of paper side by side.

2 Try to push them apart by blowing between them.

They move together because moving air has less air pressure than the surrounding air.

15

Barometers

Barometers measure changes in air pressure. This is a good way to predict changes in the weather.

Make a bottle barometer

You will need:

◆ a clear plastic bottle ◆ tape ◆ a strip of paper, 1 inch wide, 2 inches long ◆ a ruler ◆ a brick ◆ a shallow bowl, half-filled with water

1 Mark the paper strip every ¼ inch for two inches. Tape it onto the bottle.

2 Fill the bottle three-quarters full with water.

3 Put your finger over the top of the bottle. Turn the bottle upside down and stand it in the bowl of water. Take your finger off the end.

4 Tape the bottle to the brick to keep it from falling over.

5 Compare the water level in the bottle over a few days.

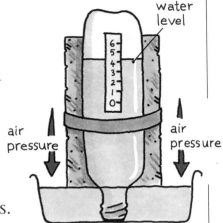

When the air pressure is high, the water in the bottle will rise.

When it is low, the water will fall.

Reading barometers

Most barometers have a pointer that tells you what the previous pressure was. Note the pressure reading on your barometer each day.

Sudden changes toward low pressure indicate storms approaching.

Rising pressure indicates dry weather.

Steadily falling pressure indicates wet and windy weather.

Reading weather maps

Areas of low pressure are called depressions and consist of warm, moist, light air that is rising. Areas of high pressure are called anticyclones and have heavy, cold, dry air that is sinking.

You will need:

◈ several days of weather maps from newspapers

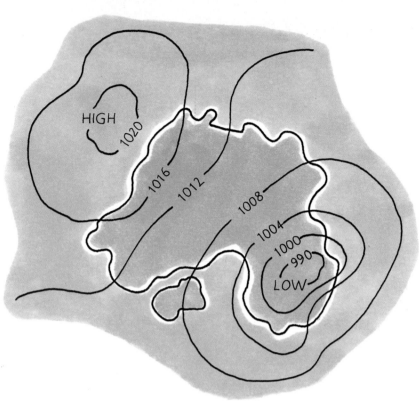

1 Find the **isobars**. These are lines that join places with the same air pressure.

2 Find a **warm front**.

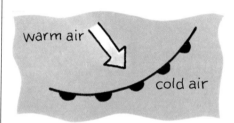

This happens where the warm air of a depression rides up over the cold air.

200 miles of rain or snow

3 Find a **cold front**.

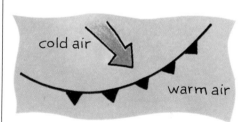

This happens when the cold air pushes under the warm air.

50 miles of rain or snow

4 Find an area on the map that is under a front.

5 Forecast the weather for that area. Compare your forecast to the one written beside the map.

A warm front brings stratus clouds and steady rain. A cold front brings towering cumulonimbus thunderclouds, showers, and then clear, bright weather.

Wind direction

Make a weather vane

You will need:

◆ a plastic flower pot filled with sand
◆ a pencil ◆ a cork ◆ tape ◆ a straw
◆ a small, tapered piece of cardboard ◆ a pin
◆ a thimble ◆ a small bead ◆ scissors

1 Tape the cork to the top of the pencil and push the pencil into the sand.

2 Make a 1-inch lengthwise cut into the straw. Push the cardboard into the cut to make a tail.

3 Find the balance point of the straw by balancing it on your finger.

4 Using the thimble, carefully push the pin through the balance point of the straw, then through the bead and into the cork. (The bead will help the straw move easily.)

5 Take the weather vane outside.

In which direction does it point?

> A southerly wind blows from the south.
>
> A northerly wind blows from the north.

What causes wind?

Wind blows from high-pressure areas to low-pressure areas. Big differences in the pressure between areas cause strong winds.

What effect do buildings have?

You will need:

◆ a weather vane
◆ a notebook and pencil
◆ a magnetic compass

1 Sketch a simple map of your school or home.

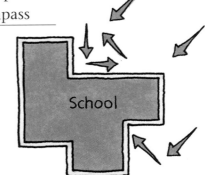

2 Use your weather vane and compass to test the wind direction in various places.

3 Show the wind directions on your map using arrows.

Buildings cause eddies, or whirls, in the wind. To get a true wind direction, your weather vane would need to be out in the open, away from buildings.

Most common wind direction

You will need:

◆ a weather vane (from page 18) ◆ a pencil
◆ a magnetic compass ◆ a notebook

1 Copy this wind rose graph into your notebook.

2 Use your weather vane to tell you the wind direction.

3 Shade in a square each day showing the wind direction.

4 Which is the most common wind direction?

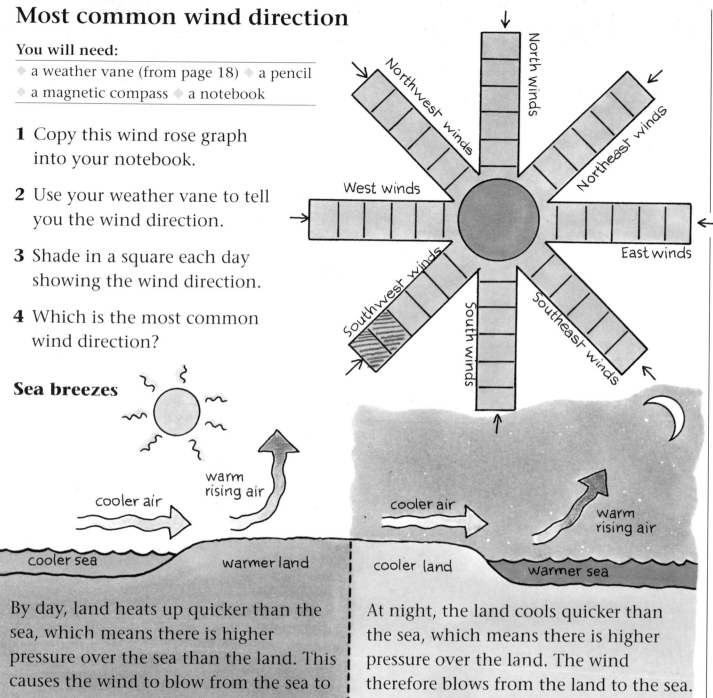

Sea breezes

By day, land heats up quicker than the sea, which means there is higher pressure over the sea than the land. This causes the wind to blow from the sea to the land. This is called a sea breeze.

At night, the land cools quicker than the sea, which means there is higher pressure over the land. The wind therefore blows from the land to the sea.

Mountain winds

Mountains divert wind up and over them and down the other side. The winds cool as they rise and warm as they fall. The Chinook is a warm, dry wind that blows down the eastern slopes of the Rocky Mountains.

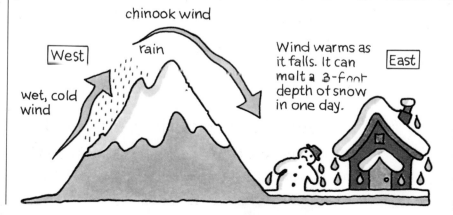

chinook wind

West

rain

wet, cold wind

Wind warms as it falls. It can melt a 3-foot depth of snow in one day.

East

Wind speed

Make an anemometer

You will need:

◆ a table-tennis ball ◆ a protractor
◆ tape ◆ thread ◆ a ruler

1 Tape a piece of thread to the table-tennis ball.

2 With the straight edge of the protractor upward, tape the other end of the thread to the middle of the protractor.

3 Tape the ruler along the top of the protractor to make a handle.

4 Holding the **anemometer** by the handle, point it into the wind, making sure the protractor is level.

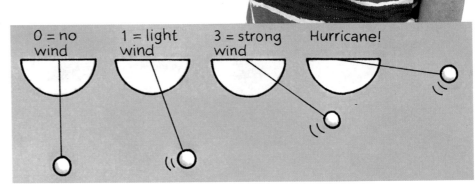

5 What angle do the ball and thread make on the protractor? This is a measurement of wind speed.

6 Keep a record of the approximate wind speed. The greater the angle, the higher the wind speed.

Did you know?

The fastest wind speed ever recorded was 231 miles per hour on Mount Washington in New Hampshire.

Hurricanes

Hurricanes are formed over warm oceans when winds blowing from opposite directions start a spiral of warm, wet air.

Hurricanes are also called cyclones, typhoons, and willy-willies in different parts of the world.

Make a propeller

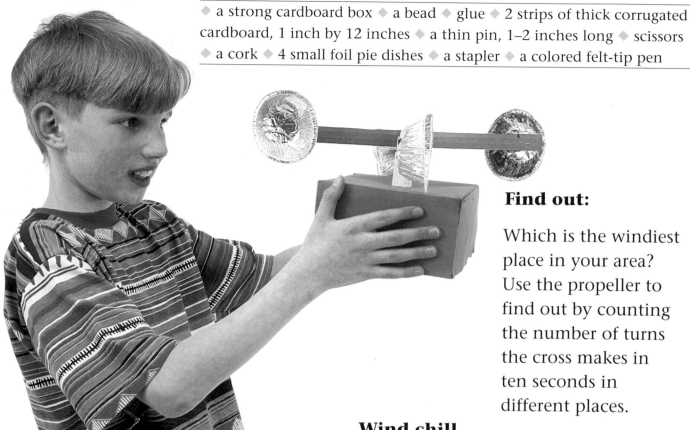

You will need:

◆ a strong cardboard box ◆ a bead ◆ glue ◆ 2 strips of thick corrugated cardboard, 1 inch by 12 inches ◆ a thin pin, 1–2 inches long ◆ scissors ◆ a cork ◆ 4 small foil pie dishes ◆ a stapler ◆ a colored felt-tip pen

1 Glue the cork to the top of the box.

2 At the center of each corrugated strip, cut into half the width of each.

3 Slot the cuts into one another to make a cross.

4 Staple a foil dish to each arm of the cross. Make sure the dishes all face the same way.

5 Color one dish with the felt-tip pen.

6 Carefully push the pin through the center of the cross, through the bead, and into the cork. The bead will make the cross spin easily.

Find out:

Which is the windiest place in your area? Use the propeller to find out by counting the number of turns the cross makes in ten seconds in different places.

Wind chill

Strong winds cool you by blowing away heat. If the ground temperature was 32 °F, it would feel like 10 °F in a 15 miles per hour wind.

The Beaufort scale

Listen to weather forecasts for sailors. They mention the wind force. This is the Beaufort scale for wind speeds.

Force 1: Light air
Force 5: Fresh breeze
Force 8: Gale
Force 12: Hurricane

Thunderstorms

What causes lightning?

Lightning is static electricity that builds up when drops of water and ice particles are blown up and down inside a big cumulonimbus cloud.

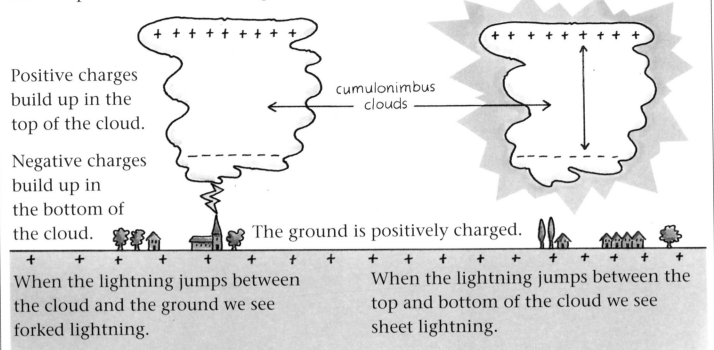

Positive charges build up in the top of the cloud.

Negative charges build up in the bottom of the cloud.

cumulonimbus clouds

The ground is positively charged.

When the lightning jumps between the cloud and the ground we see forked lightning.

When the lightning jumps between the top and bottom of the cloud we see sheet lightning.

Lightning from an electrical storm illuminates the night sky over a city.

Homemade lightning

Comb really dry, clean hair in a dark room. The sparks are miniature lightning flashes. They are caused when the plastic comb rubs against the hair, making static electricity.

How far away is the thunderstorm?

You will need:
◆ a watch with a second hand
◆ a thunderstorm (listen for warnings on the weather forecast)

1 As soon as you see a flash of lightning, start counting in seconds using your watch.

2 Stop counting as soon as you hear the **thunder**. Write down the number of seconds.

sound waves

light

Light travels faster than sound. Light from the lightning travels instantly to your eye, but the sound of the thunder only travels at 1,086 feet per second.

3 Use this speed and your second count to find out how far away the thunderstorm is.

4 About how long would it take the sound of the thunder to travel 1 mile (5,280 feet)?

a) about 3 seconds?
b) about 5 seconds?
c) about 10 seconds?

5 Count the intervals between the lightning and thunder for ten minutes.

6 Are the intervals getting shorter or longer? This tells you whether the storm is getting closer or farther away.

What should you do in a lightning storm?

- Get indoors if you can.

- If you are in an open field, crouch down.

- Keep clear of trees – they attract the lightning.

Conductor

Many tall buildings have lightning rods to conduct the lightning down to the earth. Look for pointed metal objects atop church steeples and other tall buildings. You might also see a metal strip running down the side of the building.

Sunny days

How do rainbows form?

You will need:

◆ a spray bottle filled with water

1 Spray a mist of water in the sunlight.

2 Move until you can see **rainbows** in the mist of water.

Can you see rainbows best when you are facing the sun or when the sun is behind you?

Each raindrop splits the sunlight into the colors of the spectrum.

white sunlight

raindrop

Indoor rainbows

You will need:

◇ a thick glass ashtray or a drinking glass with a thick base

◇ a glass bowl of water ◆ a mirror ◆ a sunny day

1 Put the ashtray or glass on a windowsill in the sun and move it until you create a rainbow.

2 Hold the bowl of water and mirror so that the sun shines onto the mirror through the water.

mirror

Sunshine records

Weather stations use a large glass ball to focus sunlight onto a strip of heat-sensitive paper. Meteorologists figure out the hours of sunshine each day by the length of the scorch mark on the paper. Fax paper is heat sensitive.

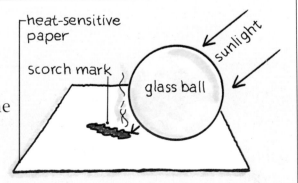

heat-sensitive paper

scorch mark

glass ball

sunlight

Make a solar heater

Your will need:

◆ a clear plastic bottle ◆ a clothespin ◆ at least 3 feet of plastic tubing (about ½ inch diameter) ◆ bath caulking ◆ a large sheet of stiff cardboard ◆ tape ◆ cold water

1 Ask an adult to make a single hole near the base of the bottle. The hole must be a little smaller than the plastic tubing.

2 Push the tubing a little way into that hole and seal it with the caulking.

3 Fill the bottle and the whole tube with cold water.

4 Put the free end of the tube into the neck of the bottle and hold it in place with the clothespin.

5 Tape the rest of the tubing flat down onto the piece of cardboard.

6 Position the cardboard in the sunlight so that only the tubing on the cardboard is in the sun.

7 Keep one hand on the bottle and find out what happens to the temperature of the water in the bottle.

Heated water in the tubing rises and circulates through the bottle.

Greenhouses

You will need:

◆ 2 thermometers ◆ a clear plastic bag

Put one of the thermometers into the plastic bag, and place both thermometers outdoors in the sun.

Which shows the higher temperature after ten minutes?

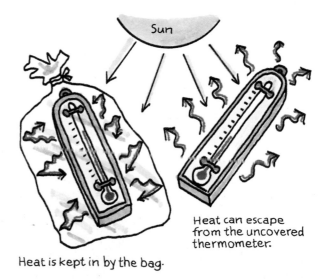

Heat can escape from the uncovered thermometer.

Heat is kept in by the bag.

Air pollution

How badly polluted is your air?

You will need:

- 3 large empty cans
- 3 sheets of white paper
- a magnifying glass

1 Roughly line the cans with white paper.

2 Put them in different places near your home or school.

3 After a week compare the papers. Use the magnifying glass to examine the specks of dirt. This is a measure of **air pollution**.

clean

on windowsill

near garden wall

near road

Air quality

Many weather forecasts include checks on the amount of air pollution.

Pollen count

Pollen is a natural air pollutant. It is the yellowy dust produced by the male parts of flowers. Pollen causes hay fever, which makes people sneeze and have red eyes. Make a survey of your friends in early summer. How many are affected by hay fever?

Not affected	Affected a little	Badly affected
✓ ✓ ✓	✓ ✓	✓ ✓
✓ ✓ ✓	✓ ✓ ✓	
✓ ✓ ✓		

Leaf check

You will need:

- 2 collections of leaves pulled off trees, one set from close to and one set from far away from a road
- 2 damp cotton balls

1 Wipe the samples from the roadside with a cotton ball.

2 Wipe the samples from far away from the road with the second cotton ball.

Which cotton ball gets dirtier?

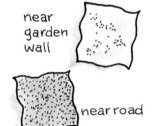

What is the effect of acid rain?

You will need:

◆ 4 flower pots filled with soil ◆ lettuce seeds
◆ vinegar ◆ measuring spoons ◆ water
◆ 8 adhesive labels ◆ 4 jam jars

1 Label the plant pots and jam jars "1," "2," "3," and "4."

2 Plant lettuce seeds in each pot.

3 Put 2 tblsp. vinegar in jar 1; 1 tblsp. vinegar and 1 tblsp. water in jar 2; 1 teasp. vinegar and 5 teasp. water in jar 3; and 2 tblsp. water in jar 4.

4 Water each pot every day for two weeks, using the liquid in jar 1 for plant pot 1, and so on. Water each pot with the same amount of liquid. Don't make the soil soaking wet.

5 Record what happens to the seedlings in each pot.

Test rainwater

Acid rain is caused when rain dissolves gases like carbon dioxide and sulfur dioxide from the air. It can cause damage to coniferous trees and stone and bricks in towns. Vinegar has an effect similar to that of acid rain.

You will need:

◆ 2 red cabbage leaves ◆ a pitcher ◆ a wooden spoon ◆ hot tap water ◆ 4 teasp. distilled water in a glass jar ◆ 4 teasp. rainwater in a glass jar

1 Tear the cabbage leaves into pieces and put them in the pitcher.

2 Add hot tap water and stir the leaves until the water turns purple.

3 Pour an equal amount of the cabbage juice into each of the jars and notice whether the juice changes color.

If the rainwater turns red, it is acid.

Weather forecasting

You will need:
◆ a rain gauge (page 6)
◆ a thermometer (page 8)
◆ a barometer (page 16)
◆ a weather vane (page 18)
◆ an anemometer (page 20)

1 Draw a weather chart like this.

2 Test the weather each morning for a week using your equipment and put your results in the chart.

3 After a week, use this information to help you forecast the weather for the same day and the next day.

	Mon	Tues	Wed	Thur	Fri	Sat	Sun
Rainfall amount (inches)							
Cloud — Amount							
Cloud — Type							
Atmospheric pressure (inches)							
Temperature (°F)							
Wind speed (angle on protractor)							
Wind direction (N, S, E, or W)							
Sunshine — bright							
Sunshine — dull							

Remember:

- Falling air pressure usually means rain is coming.

- Rising air pressure usually means fine weather.

- Northerly winds in the northern hemisphere and southerly winds in the southern hemisphere mean it will probably get colder.

Make a television forecast

You will need:
- today's newspaper ◆ a large sheet of paper
- scissors ◆ glue ◆ colored pencils

1 Look at the weather map of the country in the newspaper. Look for isobars, warm and cold fronts, and pressure areas. Look at the symbols for temperature, wind speed, and wind direction.

2 Make a large outline of the country on the sheet of paper and cut it out.

3 Make weather symbols for sun, rain, and clouds like the ones below.

wind speed and direction

temperature

fine

cloudy

rain

snow

4 Glue symbols onto the map, forecasting the weather for tonight.

5 Present a weather forecast to your friends using your weather map and symbols.

Tree rings

You will need:
- a tree stump or a log showing growth rings

1 Look at the rings. Each pair of dark and light rings shows a year's growth.

- Wide rings show a good growing year – it was probably warm and damp.

- Narrow rings show a bad growing year – it was probably cold and dry.

2 Count backward. What was the weather like in the year you were born?

Birthday weather

What's your favorite kind of weather? Visit your local library and look at newspapers from the day your were born. Was the weather on your birthday the kind you like?

Glossary

Air masses Huge areas of air that come from different parts of the world and are named after the kind of climate they come from.

Air pollution Gases or solid pieces in the air produced by burning fuels, which make air harmful in some way.

Air pressure The pressing of air in all directions. Air pressure decreases with height. Cold air has a greater air pressure than warm air.

Anemometer A device that measures wind speed.

Cold front A change from warm to cold air. There is often rain at a cold front as the cold air cools the warm wet air it is in contact with.

Condense Change from a gas to a liquid.

Convection currents Movements of warm air upward and cooler air downward.

Frost Frozen drops of dew on the ground, grass, or trees.

Hail Frozen raindrops.

Isobars Lines on weather maps that join those areas where the air pressure at sea level is the same over a period of time (such as 24 hours).

Lightning A large spark which jumps between clouds or from clouds to the ground.

Meteorologist A person who studies the earth's atmosphere, especially concerning weather and climate.

Precipitation Rain, sleet, hail, or snow.

Rainbow Bands of different-colored light seen in the sky, caused when sunlight is broken up into the colors of the spectrum by drops of water in the air.

Thermometer A device for measuring temperature.

Thunder The noise made by a flash of lightning.

Troposphere The lowest layer of the atmosphere in which weather clouds occur.

Warm front A change from cold to warm air. There is often rain at a warm front, because the cold air condenses the water vapor in the warm, wet air.

Weather vane An arrow that points in the direction from which the wind is blowing. Also called a wind vane.

Water vapor Water as an invisible gas.

Books to read

Bright, Michael. *The Greenhouse Effect.* World About Us. New York: Gloucester Press, 1991.

Bright, Michael. *The Ozone Layer.* World About Us. New York: Gloucester Press, 1991.

Davies, Key and Oldfield, Wendy. *The Super Science Book of the Weather.* Super Science. Thomson Learning, 1993.

Flint, David. *The World's Weather.* Young Geographer. New York: Thomson Learning, 1993.

Palmer, Joy. *Snow and Ice.* First Starts. Milwaukee: Raintree Steck-Vaughn, 1992.

Palmer, Joy. *Wind.* First Starts. Milwaukee: Raintree Steck-Vaughn, 1992.

Waterlow, Julia. *Flood.* Violent Earth. New York: Thomson Learning, 1993.

Wood, Jenny. *Storm.* Violent Earth. New York: Thomson Learning, 1993.

Chapter notes

Pages 4–5   Clouds form whenever warm, damp air is cooled. This cooling can take place as the air is forced to rise over hills and mountains, or when warm, wet air is in contact with cold air, as in warm and cold fronts. If the cooling is sufficient, the droplets of water in the cloud become larger and eventually precipitate as rain or snow. The size of the glass in the clouds activity is not important.

Pages 6–7   Using a narrow measuring device exaggerates the amount of rain collected. This gives good contrasts between the rainfall amounts on different days. The correct way to measure rainfall is to use a measuring cylinder that has exactly the same diameter as the rain gauge.

Pages 8–9   A sunny day will give the greatest temperature variation. If there are no clouds, in the evening the heat that has built up during the day is radiated out into space. This is why there are low temperatures on clear nights. In contrast, cloudy skies prevent heat escaping from the earth's surface, so there may be very little difference between day and night temperatures.

Pages 10–11   If you have frost where you live, examine the effects of the first frosts of the season on the plant life. Each snowflake crystallizes into a unique shape which is a variation on a hexagon.

Pages 12–13   The food coloring in the can is to show that the beads of condensation on the outside of the can are from the water in the air, not from inside the can. If the air is particularly damp, then the dew point will occur at a higher temperature than when the air is dry.

Pages 14–15   It is important to recognize that air pressure works in all directions, not just downward like gravity. The weight of the water pushing down on the cardboard is less than the air pressure pushing up on it. The way that the two pieces of paper come together is called the Bernoulli effect and explains how airplane wings gain lift.

Pages 16–17   Changes in air pressure are one of the main pieces of evidence that helps a meteorologist make a forecast. Low pressure almost always brings unsettled weather, but it is the change from relatively high to relatively low pressure that signals the arrival of a depression (another name for a low-pressure area). The numerical readings are less important than the direction and speed of change in the barometer.

Pages 18–19   Buildings cause eddies and swirls in the wind direction. Tall buildings also increase the wind speed. The Chinook is similar to the Foehn wind, which blows in the European Alps. In New Zealand the Foehn wind type is called a Nor-Wester and in Argentina it is called a Zonda. All these winds get warmer as they descend mountain ranges. Geographers call this a katabatic effect.

Pages 20–21   Hurricanes need energy from warm sea to start and maintain them. Once over land they gradually fade away. Inside the eye of a large hurricane the pressure is very low. Remnants of tropical storms drift into higher, colder latitudes as deep depressions.

Pages 22–23   Lightning storms happen most often during hot weather. The heat provides the energy that drives the strong upward winds. These winds blow pieces of ice and rain inside the cloud, which produces the static electricity.

Pages 24–25   The paper used in most fax machines is similar to that used in sunshine recorders. The solar heater works when sunshine heats the water in the tube. This water rises and enters the bottle at the top. Cold water from the bottom of the bottle replaces the warm water. The temperature of the water after about one hour will give you an indication of the strength of the sun. In many hot countries solar heating is an important form of renewable energy.

Pages 26–27   The meteorological conditions have a strong effect on the level of air pollution. Strong winds associated with depressions disperse pollutants, while the stable air of anticyclones (high pressure) concentrates the pollution over cities. Temperature inversions, where warm air layers are trapped near the ground with colder air above, trap pollutants even more. Automobiles are the main polluter in most cities.

Pages 28–29   Use the evidence from barometer readings to predict weather. A falling barometer indicates rain on the way and a rising barometer indicates fine weather. The direction of the wind is also important, with northerly winds in the northern hemisphere indicating that temperatures are likely to fall. Look for combinations and patterns using a computer database. Matching sets of tree rings from dead and fossilized trees have been used to produce accurate climate records for the last 10,000 years.

Index